Mechanical
HARRY
and the flying bicycle

For a free color catalog describing Gareth Stevens' list of high-quality books and
multimedia programs, call 1-800-542-2595 (USA) or 1-800-461-9120 (Canada).
Gareth Stevens Publishing's Fax: (414) 225-0377.

Library of Congress Cataloging-in-Publication Data

Kerr, Bob.
     Mechanical Harry and the flying bicycle / by Bob Kerr.
        p. cm.
     Summary: When he receives a call from his grandmother
asking him to come over to chop wood for her, an inventive
young boy begins a series of adventures that test his
mechanical know-how.
     ISBN 0-8368-2444-X (lib. bdg.)
     [1. Inventions—Fiction. 2. Adventures and adventurers—Fiction.
3. Cartoons and comics.] I. Title.
PN6727.K46M43 1999
741.5'973—dc21   99-19162

This North American edition first published in 1999 by
Gareth Stevens Publishing
1555 North RiverCenter Drive, Suite 201
Milwaukee, WI 53212 USA

First published in 1999 in New Zealand by Mallinson Rendel Publishers Ltd.
Original © 1999 by Bob Kerr.

Printed in Mexico

1 2 3 4 5 6 7 8 9 03 02 01 00 99

Mechanical
HARRY
and the flying bicycle

BOB KERR

Gareth Stevens Publishing
MILWAUKEE

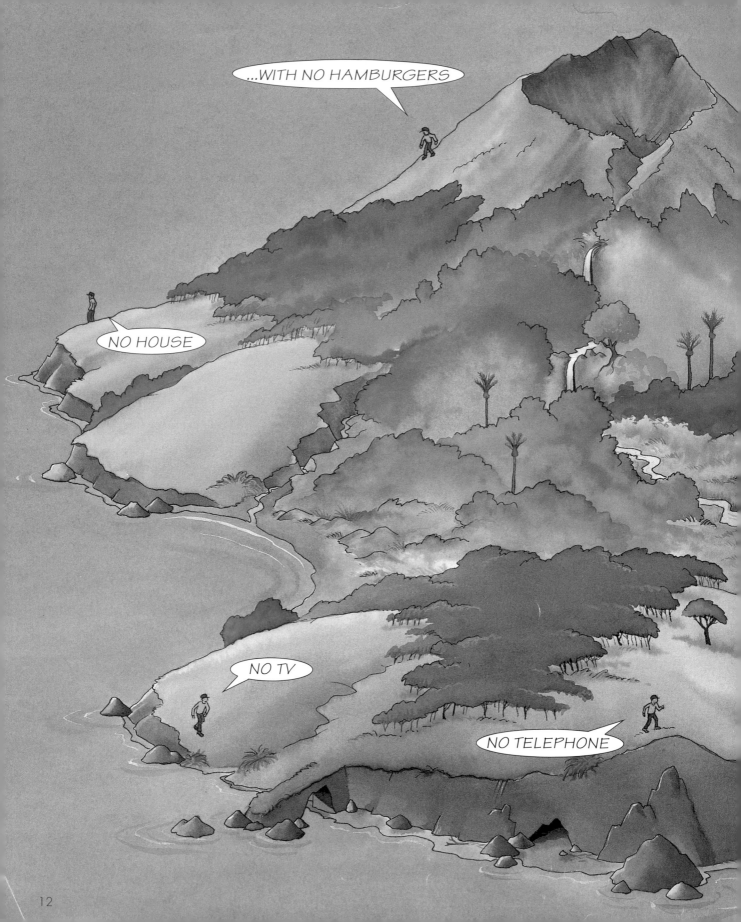

19

WE NEED MORE PLAYERS ON THE TEAM, CAT

IT'S TIME WE WERE MOVING ON

BUT WE'RE PURRRRFECTLY HAPPY HERE

WE DON'T HAVE A BALLOON, SO WE'LL HAVE TO TRY WINGS. YOU CAN TRAVEL IN MY BACKPACK

I'M NOT LEAVING!

WHOOOOSH!

The thing Harry wanted most on his journey was a Popsicle.
There are fourteen different-flavored Popsicles hidden in the story.
Can you find them?

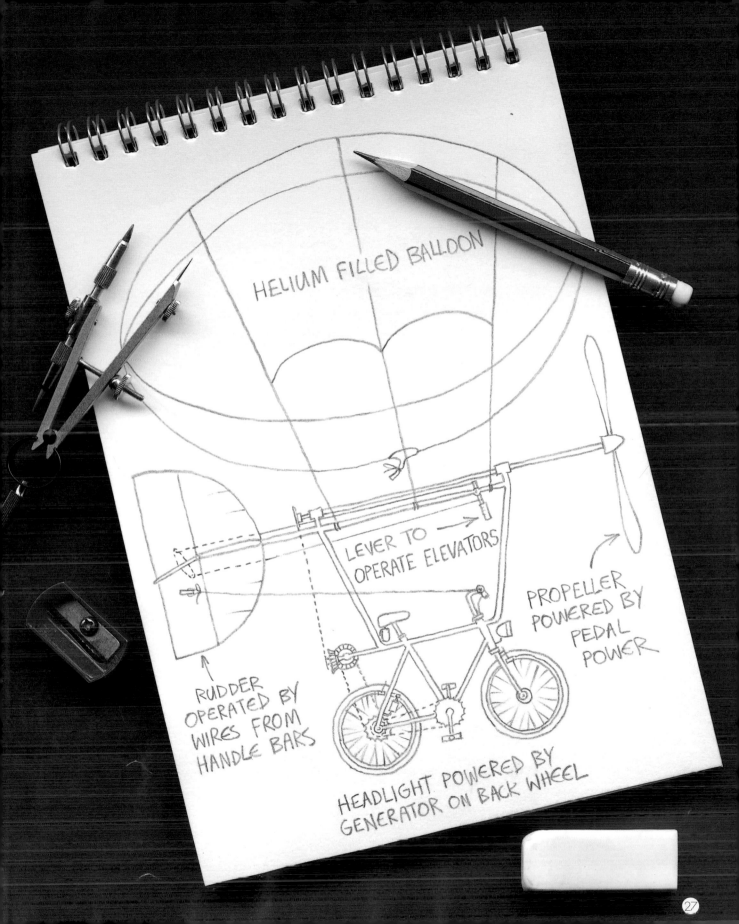

HELIUM FILLED BALLOON

LEVER TO OPERATE ELEVATORS

PROPELLER POWERED BY PEDAL POWER

RUDDER OPERATED BY WIRES FROM HANDLE BARS

HEADLIGHT POWERED BY GENERATOR ON BACK WHEEL